STELLA

QUEEN OF THE SNOW

MARIE-LOUISE GAY

A GROUNDWOOD BOOK   DOUGLAS & McINTYRE   TORONTO VANCOUVER BUFFALO

Copyright © 2000 by Marie-Louise Gay
First paperback edition 2001

All rights reserved. No part of this book may be reproduced or transmitted in any form or
by any means, without the prior written permission of the publisher or, in the case of
photocopying or other reprographic copying, a licence from CANCOPY (Canadian
Reprography Collective), Toronto, Ontario.

Groundwood Books / Douglas & McIntyre Ltd.
720 Bathurst Street, Suite 500, Toronto, Ontario M5S 2R4

Distributed in the U.S.A. by Publishers Group West
1700 Fourth Street, Berkeley, CA 94710

We acknowledge the financial support of the Canada Council for the Arts, the Ontario
Arts Council and the Government of Canada through the Book Publishing Industry
Development Program for our publishing activities.

National Library of Canada Cataloguing in Publication Data
Gay, Marie-Louise
Stella, queen of the snow

"A Groundwood book".
ISBN 0-88899-404-4 (bound) ISBN 0-88899-451-6 (pbk.)
I. Title.
PS8563.A868S728 2001   jC813'.54   C00-930208-5
PZ7.G39St 2001

Printed and bound in China by Everbest Printing Co. Ltd.

To David

Sam had never seen snow.
This was his first snowstorm.

"Isn't it beautiful, Sam?" asked Stella.
"It is very white," said Sam, "and it makes me sort of dizzy."
"Come on, Sam," said Stella. "Let's go outside."

"Is the snow cold?" asked Sam. "Is it hard and icy?"
"Snow is as cold as vanilla ice cream," answered Stella,
"and as soft as baby rabbit fur."

"Can you eat a snowflake?" asked Sam.
"Polar bears do," said Stella.
"They eat snowflakes for breakfast."

"With milk?" asked Sam.
"Yes," said Stella. "And sugar."

"Let's make a snowman, Sam," said Stella.
"Where does a snowman sleep?" asked Sam.
"In a soft, fluffy snowbank," answered Stella.

"What does a snowman eat?" asked Sam.
"Snowballs..." sang Stella, "snow peas...and snowsuits!"

"Do snowmen eat *green* snowsuits?" asked Sam.
"No," said Stella. "They only eat pink ones."

"Are you sure?" asked Sam.
"Let's go skating on the pond," said Stella.

"Where is the water?" asked Sam.
"The water is frozen," said Stella, "like a giant silver popsicle."

"Are the frogs frozen, too?" asked Sam.
"No," said Stella. "They are sleeping under the ice."

"Come on, Sam," said Stella. "Put on your skates."

"Not right now," said Sam. "I'm listening to the frogs snore."

"Hey!" said Sam. "Why is fog coming out of my mouth?"
"When it's this cold," said Stella, "your words freeze.
Every word has a different fog shape. See?"

"I can't read yet," said Sam.
"Then let's build a fort," said Stella.

"Where does snow come from?" asked Sam.
"Where does snow go in the summer?
How many snowflakes are there in a snowball?"

"I don't know, Sam," sighed Stella. "Come and help me."
"Just a minute," said Sam. "I'm counting the snowflakes..."

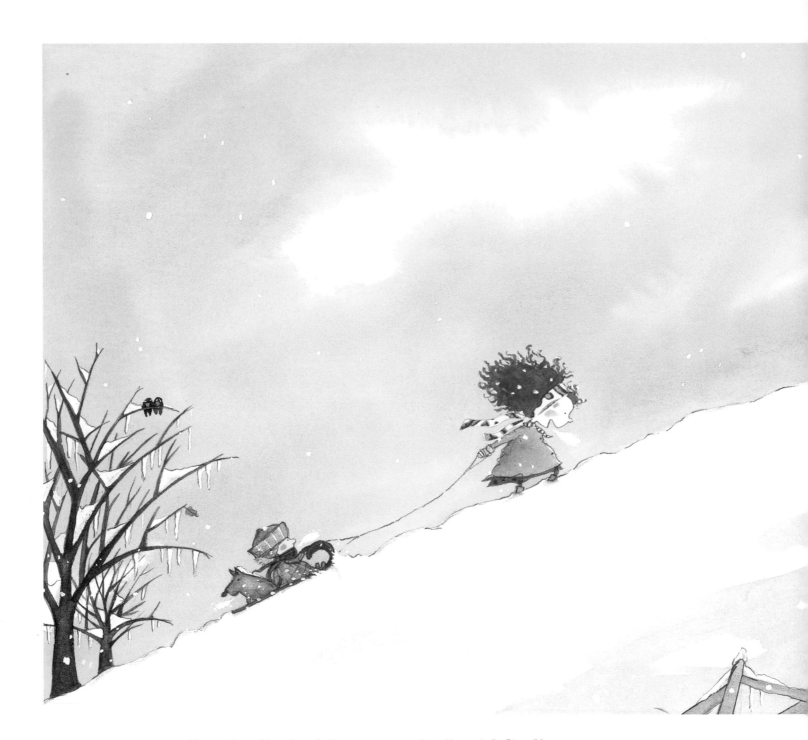

"Let's climb this mountain," said Stella.
"Why?" said Sam. "What for?"
"Then we'll slide down," said Stella.

"Will we go very fast?" asked Sam.
"Faster than a bird," sang Stella.
"Faster than an airplane."

"Will we be able to stop?" asked Sam.
"Stop?" said Stella. "Who wants to stop? Hop on!"

"I think I'll walk down," said Sam.

"Do dogs get cold?" asked Sam.
"No," said Stella. "Dogs wear fur coats."
"Do birds get goosebumps?" asked Sam.

"No," said Stella. "Birds wear snowboots."
"Like mine?" asked Sam.
"Yes," said Stella, "only much smaller."

"Let's make snow angels," said Stella,
"with wide feathery wings."

"Do snow angels fly?" asked Sam.
"Do snow angels sing?"

"Of course," said Stella. "Can't you hear them?"

"Yes!" whispered Sam.